ZAC POWER

MIND GAMES
BY H.I. LARRY

ILLUSTRATIONS BY CRAIG PHILLIPS

hardie grant EGMONT

CHAPTER 1

One afternoon, Zac Power was shopping for cool new sneakers at Westbridge Mall.

Zac was a bit of an expert on the subject of being cool. He was 12 years old, and he worked as a spy for the Government Investigation Bureau, or GIB for short.

As he shopped, Zac watched out for people he knew. He didn't want anyone from school to think he cared how he looked. That would be try-hard.

At Hot Diggity, the hot-dog shop, Ann and her best friend Lucy were giggling into their milkshakes. Girls!

His favourite CD shop, Tunez, was full of kids from school. The whole world seemed to be hanging out at Westbridge. But Zac slipped by them all, unnoticed.

Zac headed towards Sports Station. Inside, the music was so loud the walls were shaking. It was rock music, the only kind Zac liked. Sports Station had the best sneakers at Westbridge. Zac's favourites were a pair with green and yellow stripes on the side.

Zac picked them up. Straight away, a sales guy bounced over. A plastic name tag on a cord around his neck read, 'Davo'.

'You all right, mate?' asked Davo.

'Can I try these? Size…uh…eight?' Zac said.

'No worries. I'll go check out the back.'

The sales guy disappeared into the storeroom. Zac waited. He looked at some T-shirts. No sales assistant. He picked up a magazine and checked out the photos of kids in the latest clothes skateboarding down stair-rails. Still no Davo.

What is he doing out there?

Suddenly, Davo reappeared, a shoebox in his hand and a weird look on his face.

'We didn't have size eight in the green and yellow. But why don't you try these on instead?'

He opened the box. Inside, Zac saw a pair of the ugliest sneakers *ever*. They were grey, the colour of belly-button fluff. The soles were twice as thick as ordinary sneakers. They were covered in wires and flashing lights.

'Nah, that's OK, thanks,' said Zac, heading for the door.

'Come on! They're limited edition. I guarantee no-one else'll have a pair like them.'

Zac rolled his eyes. 'No-one would want to!'

Davo pulled the grey sneakers out of the box.

'Just try 'em.'

Heaving a big sigh, Zac grabbed the shoes and pulled them on. They felt even worse than they looked!

As soon as his foot was inside, clamps grabbed Zac's ankles. He stood up and couldn't help wobbling as he took a step. Each sneaker must have weighed about 100 kilos.

'What do you think?' asked Davo.

Zac shook his head. 'I might wait 'til you get the others in.'

'Oh, come on, Zac. Just take them.'

Zac? How did this guy know his name?

Davo leant over to pick up the box. His name tag flipped over and Zac caught a glimpse of the back.

Was it? Yes, it was! The GIB crest!

Davo grabbed Zac by the arm and whispered in his ear, 'They're yours, OK? Now get out of here.'

Before Zac could stop him, Davo disappeared with Zac's old sneakers. Great! Now Zac had to walk all the way home in the weird grey sneakers.

He stepped out of Sports Station. Ann and Lucy had finished their milkshakes and gone home. Perhaps he was safe...

Then...

KERR-BOOOOOM!

There was an ear-splitting explosion. A cloud of white smoke. The gross grey sneakers had exploded!

Zac shot up off the ground. He flew through the air, propelled by his exploding sneakers. They had the force of ten rockets. No, make that 100 rockets!

Zac shot past Hot Diggity. Tunez was a blur. He was flying towards a set of lifts. The metal doors were closed. Yikes! He was going to smash right into them.

At the very last second, the lift doors opened and suddenly, Zac was falling. He looked up and saw the lift stuck high above him. He was falling straight down the lift well.

Round and round, faster and faster he fell in a mid-air forward roll.

At the bottom of the lift well, Zac landed with a thud on hard, cold concrete. Lucky he had been taught how to land safely during GIB training, or he would have broken a bone for sure.

The lift doors opened with a ping.

Zac was in an underground car park. Parked nearby was a white van with a satellite dish on the top. The door opened and a strong pair of arms dragged Zac into the back.

The door slammed shut and, with a screech of tyres, the van took off.

Zac looked down at his feet. The

exploding sneakers were totally gone. All that was left was a very holey, smoky pair of socks.

'Hello, Zac,' said the strong-armed man, who was driving the van. 'I've been expecting you.'

CHAPTER 2

'I'm Agent-In-Training Gorman, GIB Transport Division,' said the man. 'Hope that wasn't too uncomfortable, Zac,' he went on, looking guiltily at Zac's socks. 'I've just transferred from Stationery and Supplies, actually. You're my first agent pick-up.'

Zac remembered his first mission.

He smiled at Gorman. It wasn't easy being the new guy.

'Do you know the way to the airport, Zac?' asked Gorman.

'The airport? Why? What's my mission?' said Zac.

Gorman fished around in his pockets. 'It's somewhere in here,' muttered Gorman to himself.

At last he found what he was looking for. He handed Zac a small metal disc.

Zac loaded the disc into his SpyPad. Every GIB spy had a SpyPad. It looked sort of like an electronic game, but really it was a tablet with in-built GPS, laser and code-breaking apps, all rolled into one.

CLASSIFIED
MISSION INITIATED 9 A.M.

Unknown hostiles are hacking into the computer system controlling GIB's satellite system, WorldEye. WorldEye is so powerful it can read a newspaper headline from 500 kilometres up. The software is protected by encrypted passwords and high-level firewalls. Still, the hackers have managed to breach every firewall but one.

YOUR MISSION
- Locate hackers.
- Discover why they want to hack into WorldEye.
- Prevent breaching of final firewall

~ END ~

This was bad!

Only one firewall standing between WorldEye and a bunch of criminals!

'What does Leon think?' asked Zac, as the van turned onto the freeway to the airport.

Leon, Zac's brother, was a Technical Support Officer with GIB. If anyone knew how to handle computer hackers, it was Leon.

'Leon's tracked the hackers to the city of Bladesville,' said Gorman.

Zac fought back a proud smile. Sometimes nerdy brothers really did come in handy.

'You wouldn't be smiling if you knew

anything about Bladesville,' said Gorman. His eyes widened. 'I've heard it's one of the meanest, toughest, dirtiest cities in the whole world.'

Zac said nothing. Whatever Bladesville had in store for him, he could deal with it. Couldn't he?

'Oh, yeah,' Gorman went on. 'Leon reckons it'll take the hackers 24 hours to breach the last firewall.'

Only 24 hours? Zac did some quick calculations in his head.

Now he was freaking out!

'Says here the mission started at 9 a.m. today, so that means I've only got until 9 a.m. tomorrow to fly to Bladesville and stop the hackers. And it's – ' Zac glanced at his SpyPad – 'already 6.51p.m.!'

Gordon looked guilty for a moment.

'Yeah, sorry about the delay in getting you on the mission, Zac. First time and everything, you see.'

Gorman coughed nervously. But Zac could see there wasn't any point getting angry. Gorman was doing the best he could. Was it his fault his best was, um, not really very good?

Gorman opened the van's glovebox.

'I nearly forgot these,' he said, passing Zac a pair of wraparound glasses with a slick-looking computer game controller attached.

'These aren't going to explode, are they?' Zac asked, thinking of the sneakers.

'No, they're virtual-reality glasses,' said Gorman vaguely.

Zac put the glasses on.

It looked exactly like he was sitting in the cockpit of a fighter jet. Zac grabbed the controller. Through the glasses, it looked like he was touching real fighter-jet controls.

'Woah!' said Zac. It was the most realistic flight simulator he had ever seen.

'Isn't it incredible?' said Gorman. 'Ever piloted a fighter-jet before?'

Zac hadn't, but he couldn't wait to try. He took hold of the steering yoke. He sped off down the tarmac. He engaged the throttle. Then, with a loud, realistic whoosh of air, he was airborne!

Up Zac flew. He burst through the clouds. He was 20,000 feet and climbing fast.

He fiddled with the controls. One was for speed, one was to turn left and right. *This flying thing isn't so hard,* thought Zac.

Then Zac heard a warning siren.

A message flashed on his virtual computer screen.

...STORM ALERT!...

The sky went dark. Purple lightning slashed the sky. The plane shook violently. Zac's fighter had been struck!

The jet jerked one way, then the other. Zac couldn't get control of the steering. His computer screen flashed again.

...LOSING ALTITUDE!...

The plane nose-dived.

Helpless, Zac watched the altitude drop from 20,000 to 10,000 feet in a few seconds. He broke through the clouds. Right below was a mountain range. He was going to crash!

Zac winced and braced himself for impact. The fighter spun onto its back and slammed into the mountains. It burst into flames.

...GAME OVER! YOU LOSE!...

Zac ripped off the virtual-reality glasses.

He was sweating. The plane crash had felt so real!

'All right, Zac?' asked Gorman.

Zac nodded.

'Computer games are so advanced these days,' Gorman continued. 'And so addictive! They really play mind games with you.'

Ghost-white, Zac nodded.

'Well, don't worry. We're at the airport now,' said Gorman cheerfully.

The van turned into a secret side entrance. The tarmac was just ahead. And there, waiting for Zac, was a miniature fighter jet.

'Probably should've told you before,'

said Gorman, absent-mindedly. 'You're flying yourself to Bladesville. The flight simulator was your training.'

Zac said nothing.

A spy always keeps his cool.

'That's OK with you, isn't it, Zac?'

CHAPTER

Zac strode casually across the tarmac towards the mini-fighter jet. He raced up the stairs to the cockpit. The controls looked almost the same as the ones in the flight simulator. A radio headset sat on the pilot's seat.

Zac put it on and heard a voice.

'Zac Power, this is Air Traffic Control.

The time is 8.09 p.m. Weather conditions fine. You're cleared for take-off on runway three.'

Zac took hold of the yoke. He engaged the throttle and the engine growled.

The fighter jet taxied across the tarmac. Zac angled the yoke upwards and pushed harder on the throttle. The jet gathered speed. Then, with a loud thump as the wheels folded up, Zac was in the air.

But this time, it was for real!

Steadily, Zac climbed. He pierced the clouds. The sun was out and there was no wind. Perfect flying conditions!

Zac tipped the yoke forward. The plane dipped down. He pulled the yoke up again.

The plane shot upwards. He pulled the yoke sharp right. The jet flipped over onto its side!

Cool! Zac tried the left-hand side. He shot into a wicked loop-the-loop.

Maybe this wasn't getting him to Bladesville as fast as possible. But it was *so* worth it!

A voice crackled in Zac's radio headset.

'Come in, Zac Power.'

'Power here,' said Zac, as confidently as he could.

'Weather conditions in your airspace have declined,' said Air Traffic Control. 'A freak electrical storm's heading your way.'

Zac looked around. The brilliant sunshine had gone. Heavy black clouds were everywhere.

The fighter started to rattle and bump. Turbulence!

'Suggest emergency landing,' said Air Traffic Control.

Zac looked at the time.

10.48 P.M.

If Zac landed now, it'd take him for-ever to get to Bladesville and find those hackers. Freak storm or not, Zac was going to have to keep flying.

'Request permission to continue to Bladesville,' said Zac.

There was silence from Air Traffic Control. The fighter roared into a really rough air pocket. The entire cockpit shook. For a second, radio communication dropped out.

The radio came back on. 'Permission granted. Proceed at your own risk.'

Grimly, Zac flew on. Wind rattled the windscreen. The plane lifted and dropped in the wind.

It was worse than a fun-park ride.

The fighter was equipped with rocket-assisted ejector seats. Zac checked where the lever was, just in case.

Beside the lever, Zac noticed a button labelled 'Vertical Supersonic'.

Zac took a deep breath. Could this button possibly do what he hoped? If it climbed at supersonic speed, there was a chance Zac could make it above the storm and out of danger.

Just then, the cockpit lit up as lightning crackled across the sky. These were the conditions that made Zac crash the simulator!

Without thinking, Zac slammed his hand down on the Vertical Supersonic button. Immediately, the fighter jet responded. The nose rose steeply until the plane was speeding straight up.

Then…

BOOOOOOOOOOM!

A sonic boom!

Zac had broken the speed of sound. He'd gone supersonic!

He streaked upwards, leaving the storm behind him. His hands shook. Going Vertical Supersonic had been as scary as it was awesome.

CHAPTER 4

Zac jammed on the brakes. He'd been flying so fast he'd hardly noticed he was almost in Bladesville.

Now he had to figure out how and where to land. He had a closer look at the instruments and dials flashing on the dashboard. He noticed a button labelled 'Engage Stealth Shield'.

Zac hit the button.

Instantly, his mini-fighter jet vanished from his radar screen. The stealth shield had turned him invisible!

Zac looked up the location of Bladesville Airport. It was 50 kilometres out of town. He checked the time.

It was already 11.34 p.m.!

Then Zac had an idea.

If his mini fighter jet was invisible, he could land wherever he wanted!

With that decided, Zac flew downwards. Skyscrapers stuck up everywhere. The streets were choked with cars and people.

The tallest skyscraper had a huge logo

on the side. MindLab. They were some kind of games company. The top of the MindLab building was going to make the perfect landing strip for an invisible mini-fighter jet.

Coming in to land, Zac couldn't help switching on the PA system, even though he was alone. This piloting stuff was pretty fun.

'Ladies and gentlemen, this is Captain Zac Power speaking.'

His landing was perfect. Not a single bump. Maybe, in another life, Zac could have been a pilot. But he had to shut those thoughts out. He was a spy. He always would be. Zac allowed himself the smallest of sighs.

Zac popped open the invisible cockpit door. He stuck his head out and looked around the top of the MindLab building. A beefy security guard was standing near the staircase from the roof into the building.

As usual, Zac had his abseiling gear in his backpack. He'd get down the quick way. Over the side of the building. All 200 storeys!

Around floor 103, Zac's SpyPad beeped. He fished about in his pocket awkwardly – abseiling a hundred floors above a busy street wasn't the perfect time to be checking messages.

It was a cryptic message from GIB Mission Control.

Go to Electric Eel Workshop

Shop 13, Dank Alley, Bladesville.

Your contact is Mrs X.

Zac made it down to the street and looked around. He'd never seen such a strange place. It was the middle of the night, but it was still burning hot. Stalls selling food and fake electronic games were everywhere. Music blasted. A monorail snaked overhead.

According to his SpyPad's GPS, Dank Alley was not far.

He zigzagged down alleys smelling of fish and rubbish. Finally, he found Dank Alley. Shop 13 was down the end, nearly hidden by steam rising up from a gutter.

A sign on the grimy door read, 'We're closed, so go away'.

Zac knocked anyway. 'Mrs X?' he called. 'It's Zac Power.'

Six or seven deadlocks opened. The door swung open a crack. In the dim light, Zac saw a woman about his own height. Her face was wrinkled, her hair white. A tattoo of an eel twisted up her arm. She looked 120 years old!

'Come,' she said in a funny accent. With a crooked old finger, she directed Zac to the back of the shop. There stood something covered with a dusty old sheet. Whatever it was, Zac couldn't imagine needing it for his mission.

Mrs X pulled off the sheet. Underneath, was a brand-new motor scooter. There were millions just like it roaring down the streets of Bladesville. Only those ones were dented and rusty. This one gleamed silver.

'One important addition,' said Mrs X. She pointed at a lever on the front. 'Pull up, you fly. Pull down, you sing karaoke.'

'This is a karaoke hover scooter?' said Zac, disbelieving. Mrs X nodded.

'You go. Tell GIB I send big bill, very soon.' Mrs X started to cackle to herself.

Zac was wheeling the scooter out into Dank Alley when his SpyPad beeped.

'You have one new voice message,' the screen flashed.

Zac put the SpyPad to his ear.

'Hello, Zac. Welcome to Bladesville,' said a voice – it sounded like a teenager.

Could this be one of the hackers? wondered Zac. The voice sounded so young. Then again, Zac and Leon were way better with technical stuff than their mum and dad. Zac's dad couldn't even work the DVD player!

The message went on. 'We've been tracking you since you took off. Wonderful thing, WorldEye. Anyway, we found your invisible fighter jet. Pretty cocky, landing on the MindLab building. If you want to live, you better get out of here. Right now.'

The hackers were onto him! And, by the sounds of things, they'd managed to gain partial control of WorldEye even without breaching the final firewall.

Zac's mission suddenly felt a lot more dangerous.

CHAPTER 5

Zac crouched in a dark doorway, hidden in shadow. He clutched his SpyPad tight. He was in a foreign city and totally alone. His hands weren't shaking, exactly. But he'd have to admit that the message from the hackers made him edgy.

He punched in the number for GIB Tech Support.

Leon picked up the phone. A friendly voice! Relief flooded through Zac.

'Listen to this message, Leon. I'll patch it through now,' said Zac.

Leon listened.

'Nasty,' he said. 'But don't worry. I'll trace the message. Could lead you straight to the hackers.'

Zac waited nervously.

Finally, Leon had something. 'The message seems to have come from somewhere within a one-kilometre radius of your current location,' he said.

It was 2.47 a.m. already. Zac had to get a move-on!

'Can't you tell me anything else?' asked

Zac. 'It'll take me weeks to search a square kilometre in this place.'

But Leon couldn't. 'They've got a very effective location-scrambling device, Zac. These hackers are pretty clued in.'

Great! That was all Zac needed to hear!

Zac wasn't sure what to do next, so he replayed the message. This time, he thought he heard something in the background. Music? Yes, it was!

He listened again.

It sounded like 'Rotten Lies' by Nemesis, one of his favourite bands. But the singing was terrible – the voice was nothing like the lead singer's.

Zac toyed with the handlebars of his

new karaoke hover scooter.

Something clicked.

Karaoke! Bladesvillians *loved* karaoke. The hackers must have sent the message from a karaoke bar.

Zac flicked his SpyPad to GPS mode.

Find karaoke bars within one kilometre from here, he typed.

A single name popped up on the screen. The Golden Eardrum Karaoke Cave. Zac jumped on his hover scooter and sped straight there.

It didn't take Zac long to find the Golden Eardrum – it had a bright purple front door and a giant rotating ear on the roof.

He needed to go in and look around without attracting attention. But he knew most of the other customers would be grown-ups. A 12-year-old on his own would really stand out in the crowd.

Then Zac remembered something.

A couple of months ago, Leon had given him a new gadget to road-test on a mission. Zac had stuffed it into his backpack and forgotten all about it.

Zac ducked into a nearby alley and pulled out the Protector Projector. The Protector Projector created incredibly realistic 3D holograms.

All Zac had to do was film himself with the Protector Projector. The Projector would then transmit a hologram of what-ever Zac was doing in the footage. It would look absolutely real!

I've got to make it look like I'm doing karaoke, thought Zac. *Then, everyone will be watching my hologram on stage while the real me can look around the Golden Eardrum.*

He looked around the alley carefully. Yes, it seemed deserted. He was going to have to film himself singing here.

Zac set the Protector Projector to Record mode. *They like Nemesis at the Golden Eardrum...better do a Nemesis song,* thought Zac.

'Drivin' down the highway, feelin' pretty cool,' Zac sang.

How embarrassing! Zac couldn't just stand there, either. To make this perform-ance look real, he'd have to dance too. Secretly, he'd always dreamt of being a rock star. Now he had to pretend he really was one!

'No place to go today, not even school,' Zac wailed, getting warmed up.

This chorus bit was actually pretty cool. Zac played a solo on the air guitar. For once, his dream of becoming a rock star and his spying missions were fitting together perfectly!

Zac hit Stop on the Protector Projector and headed for the Golden Eardrum. He was going to track down those hackers if

it was the last thing he did. And his hologram was going to put on one awesome
show!

CHAPTER

A queue snaked out of the Golden Eardrum. Men in suits shouted and swayed. Women in their best dresses teetered in high-heeled shoes.

None of these people look like hackers, thought Zac. *Actually, they look like an ad for staying at home with a good DVD.*

Just then, the bouncer unclipped the

velvet rope blocking the entrance. He waved a couple through, and Zac tagged along behind. He was inside!

The Golden Eardrum was absolutely packed. In a crowd like this, the hackers could be anywhere.

Through a smoky haze, Zac saw a stage at the front of the room. Above that, there was a large screen. Song lyrics appeared on the screen so you could follow along when you were up on stage singing.

Along one wall, he saw what looked like phone booths. They were sound-proof karaoke practice booths.

Up on stage, a trio of girls were finishing a horrible, soppy love song.

Now's my chance! Zac thought to himself. He sneaked up to the stage. He hid the Protector Projector under a nearby table and switched it on. A beam of light shot out. Zac aimed it at the stage.

Leon's gadget worked! For there, up on stage, was an absolutely realistic hologram of Zac singing a Nemesis song at the top of his voice.

The audience whistled and cheered.

Time for the real Zac to get to work!

Zac scanned the crowd. A group of teenagers stood by the stage, watching the hologram of Zac's awesome performance. *Could they be the hackers?* They looked younger than everyone else in the Golden

Eardrum. And it made sense that computer whizzes would be kids.

Just then, Zac's hologram made a strange choking noise.

What? That wasn't in the song!

'Don't wanna be a grown-up, oh no no no,' sang the hologram.

Then came the choking noise again.

'Oh no no no – '

'Oh no no no – '

The hologram was jammed! It repeated the same line over and over, like a CD skipping. Zac's cover was blown!

A second later, Zac turned back to the teenagers. But they were gone!

Then Zac saw them disappearing into

the karaoke practice booth second from the left. He counted seven people going into the booth.

That doesn't seem right, thought Zac. *How could so many kids fit into such a small space?*

Sticking to the shadows, Zac tiptoed over to the booth. He took a deep breath and threw open the door.

The booth was completely empty!

Looking down, Zac noticed a trapdoor cut into the floor.

The handle was still warm!

Zac heaved open the trapdoor. Down in the gloom, Zac saw a ladder. *Probably leads to the hackers' underground lair,* thought Zac.

Zac had no idea if the hackers would still be down there. But there was only one way to find out. As quietly as he could, Zac sneaked down the ladder.

He looked around. With its white walls and bare light bulbs, the room looked like an ordinary storeroom. The only difference was, it was filled with rows of the latest computers.

If this is the hackers' secret lair, thought Zac, *where are the hackers?*

There was absolutely no-one around.

Frustration bubbled up in Zac. He'd been so close! Yet somehow the hackers had slipped away.

Downbeat, Zac took another look

around. The hackers had left no trace behind.

No dropped wallet.

No mobile phone.

Not even a single hair.

Except…

What on earth was *that thing,* sitting on the floor?

CHAPTER 7

It was the weirdest thing Zac had ever seen. It was shaped like a normal game console, but where the left, right, up and down buttons should have been, this thing had wires hanging out. Attached to the end of the wires was a shiny metal helmet. It looked like a high-tech version of Zac's mum's colander!

Zac dug out his SpyPad and snapped a photo. Then he emailed a copy through to Tech Support back at GIB Mission Control. If there was anyone nerdy enough to know what this was, it was Leon.

A few seconds later, Zac's SpyPad rang.

'That's MindLab's latest console, the MindGame 3000!' said Leon, sounding like he was about to pop with excitement.

'What does it do?' asked Zac.

'It's like an ordinary game console, but instead of pressing buttons, you *think* your next move. You can control any computer game just with your mind!'

It sounded cool, but it wasn't going to lead Zac to the hackers.

Leon was still carrying on about the MindGame 3000. 'This is totally amazing! They're not even out on the market yet!' Leon was saying as Zac hung up.

Zac found a door at the back of the room and trailed dolefully out of the basement. He'd never let a mission defeat him before. But this time, with no real leads, he had no idea what to do next. He checked his watch.

4.23 A.M.

Time was running out.

Out in the alley, Zac hopped on his karaoke hover scooter. He was about to roar off when something caught his eye. It was a poster.

GAMES CONVENTION

Bladesville Town Hall

Try out the coolest gaming technology!

OPEN 24 HOURS

Sponsored by MindLab

Zac's spy senses zinged. *If the hackers owned a game console that wasn't even in the shops yet, wasn't it possible they'd be involved in a games convention?*

Zac was going to find out!

He zoomed through the streets of Bladesville towards the town hall. Engaging hover mode, he leapt over rubbish bins and the occasional dog. In less than ten minutes, Zac was there.

Zac stopped the hover scooter near the front entrance and raced inside. Almost immediately, he felt a hand clamp down on his shoulder.

'Excuse me, sir.'

Zac turned and saw a man in a black suit and dark sunglasses smiling grimly.

'Me?' asked Zac, as innocently as he could. He had to pretend to be an ordinary games-mad kid, not the super spy he was.

'Congratulations!' said the man, in a strange voice. 'You've won a wildcard entry into our Grand Games Battle. The best gamers in the world going head-to-head, live on the big screen.'

'Er, no thanks. I'd rather just look around the convention,' said Zac.

There were hundreds of kids milling around. The hackers were in there somewhere, Zac could feel it. He couldn't afford to waste time in some stupid games competition.

'But you've been selected by Mind-Lab, the world's most advanced gaming company. What *normal kid* would pass up a chance like that?' asked the man, his eyes narrowing. 'You are a *normal kid*, right?'

'Oh, totally normal,' said Zac hastily.

'Well, then. Step this way.'

The man slapped a hand on Zac's shoulder and shoved him towards the stage.

Two monitors and two game consoles sat waiting for the players. Overhead, a giant screen had been rigged up so everyone at the convention could see who was playing and how they were scoring.

'You know how to play *Flight Night*, right?' said the man. 'It's a flight-simulator game.' Zac shrugged. He had some experience with flight simulators...

More than most of his opponents, it seemed. One by one, Zac clobbered every challenger. It was easy. *Almost too easy,* thought Zac.

Was someone letting him win?

Pretty soon, Zac found himself in the semi-finals, leading by one point as the

siren sounded. He'd made the grand final!

Zac checked his watch.

Playing in the grand final would take up even more time. But even worse, the 8-year-old kid he'd been playing in the semis burst into tears.

'Hey, don't cry,' said Zac. 'There's always next year.'

The kid nodded, not looking convinced. The poor kid was a total *Flight Night* addict, that was obvious.

Zac gazed up at the big screen above their heads. On the screen, all you could really see of the players was the backs of their heads. The kid's hair was a totally different colour to Zac's, but maybe…

Zac grabbed a bright blue baseball cap from a nearby table of freebies.

'I've got an idea,' he said casually to the kid. 'I'm kind of in a hurry. Could you do me a favour and take my spot in the grand final?'

The kid's eyes lit up.

Zac put the cap on the kid's head. 'Just don't turn around while you're playing,' he said. 'On the screen no-one will know it's not me.

Leaving me free to look for the hackers, Zac added silently to himself.

CHAPTER

Zac leapt off the stage. Straight away, the crowd swallowed him up. He was safe, at least for the moment.

He thought over everything Leon told him about the mind-controlled game console the hackers left behind.

It was made by MindLab.

If Zac found the MindLab display here at

the Games Convention, there was a good chance the hackers would be somewhere nearby!

It wasn't hard to spot. Over in the corner, an enormous blinking neon sign read, 'MindLab. Tomorrow's gaming today.'

Zac headed over.

MindLab had set up rows of computers so everyone at the convention could try their games and equipment.

A thrill rushed through Zac. Every kid at every computer at the MindLab display was wearing a high-tech metal helmet! They were testing the MindLab 3000 console. The hackers must be very close now.

But where? Zac needed to hang back

for a while and watch. But it was already 8.01 a.m. Less than an hour until the fire-wall was breached!

The MindLab display was the most popular stand by far. Kid after kid stepped up to try out the new mind-controlled console. That made sense. *Who wouldn't want to try out something so awesome?*

All the same, Zac couldn't help thinking how rich a company like MindLab must be. *But to keep the money rolling in,* thought Zac, *they need to keep kids addicted to their games.*

Computer games were definitely fun, but there was also something a little bit creepy about the way they sucked you in.

Suddenly, Zac noticed a strange thing.

When a kid made a very high score, a man in a black suit and dark sunglasses would appear from nowhere. The man would whisper something in the kid's ear and the two of them would disappear through a door. As Zac watched, it happened three times.

Where were the men taking the games champs? And what were they whispering?

Zac dug out his trusty SpyPad. He switched it on and stuck in a pair of head-phones. The SpyPad had a high-powered multi-directional microphone feature. Zac could hear almost anything, even the softest whisper, from about 50 metres away.

Sneaking closer to the MindLab display,

Zac pointed his SpyPad at one of the men in black suits. The man leant down towards one of the kids playing.

'Hey, you're pretty good at that game,' the man said. The kid hardly looked up.

'My name's Mr Tait,' said the man, sticking out his hand. 'How'd you like a job with MindLab? We're hiring champion gamers for an interesting project we're working on. We pay good money.'

That got the kid's attention. He nodded, stood up and walked off with Mr Tait.

Zac followed along behind, as close as he dared. Mr Tait and the kid disappeared through a door that said, 'Private'.

Zac crouched down behind a pot plant

and listened. The SpyPad's microphone was so powerful, Zac could hear everything the man said, even through a closed door.

'MindLab is so much more than a gaming company,' Mr Tait was saying. 'The technology we invent for games, we also use for much bigger things. Like satellites.'

Satellites! Zac's face flushed with excitement. He was about to crack this case, he could feel it.

'At the moment, we're trying to discover how a powerful satellite called WorldEye works,' Mr Tait said. 'Since you're so good with the MindLab 3000, we thought you'd be able to help. We use the same controls for our WorldEye project, you see.'

So the kid on the other side of the door would be joining a group of kids recruited by MindLab to hack into WorldEye using the MindLab 3000. The hackers Zac followed in the karaoke bar were too!

The plan was ingenious. Develop top-level hacking technology and disguise it as an ordinary game console. Then, recruit the best gamers and pay them lots of money for their silence.

No-one would ever suspect kids would be the brains behind a plot as big as hacking into WorldEye.

Just then, the kid on the other side of the door asked Mr Tait a question.

'I thought that satellite belonged to

someone else,' the kid said. Zac held his breath. *What would Mr Tait say to that?*

There was a long silence. Then Zac heard the faintest sound. Even with the powerful SpyPad microphone, it was almost too quiet to hear. It was a cross between a sob and a whimper of pain. Zac's blood ran cold.

Zac heard Mr Tait's cruel voice. 'When you work for MindLab, you don't ever ask questions. Now you know why.'

Pins and needles prickled Zac's legs. He was going to cramp up if he didn't move soon. He shifted a millimetre to his left. But it was enough.

'Over there! Behind the pot plant!'

Oh no! One of the kids from the karaoke bar had spotted Zac.

Before he could run, Zac was surrounded. Zac recognised the man from the front entrance, the one who'd forced him to enter the games comp. He saw all the kids from the karaoke bar. And there were a whole lot of goons he hadn't met yet as well.

There was no escaping this one!

'I know someone very keen to meet you,' said the man from the front entrance in his creepy voice. He grabbed Zac roughly by the arm. 'The head of MindLab, Jimmy Shady.'

CHAPTER 9

Zac looked around for help. Surely there'd be security guards at the Games Convention? Surely they wouldn't just let a whole lot of goons march him away in broad daylight?

But then Zac remembered. MindLab was sponsoring the Games Convention. If there were security guards, they worked for MindLab. They'd be no help at all.

Zac needed a plan. But at the rate the goons were dragging him through the hall, there wasn't much time to come up with one. He'd have to think something up on the spot!

'This way,' said the man from the front entrance, yanking Zac towards a glass office overlooking the entire convention centre.

Magically, the door slid aside. There at a desk was a very short, very ugly man. His thin hair was scraped back against his skull with shiny hair gel. His skin was clammy and pocked like a toad's.

The ugly man stood up and nodded politely. It was like he and Zac were about to sit down to a friendly game of chess.

'Before I kill you,' said the ugly man, 'let me introduce myself.'

Zac knew that a spy must never show fear. Even when his stomach was flip-flopping wildly.

'I'm Jimmy Shady,' said the man. 'Take a seat. I'll tell you all about my operation.'

When he was a kid, Jimmy Shady would've been the last one picked for the footy team. The one who never got invited to anyone's birthday party. The one who ate his lunch all by himself.

Now, Zac could tell Jimmy Shady felt important at last. And he couldn't wait to tell Zac exactly how powerful he really was. In fact, Jimmy Shady was so thrilled with himself, his eyes misted over. He didn't even notice Zac unlocking his SpyPad screen. That suited Zac just fine.

'Being a GIB spy, you've no doubt worked out I'm recruiting games whizzes to help me hack into your precious World-Eye satellite.'

Zac nodded. 'Why would you want to hack into WorldEye? You're head of a games company, not an international spy,' Zac said. The more Jimmy Shady told him, the better.

'Once I control WorldEye, I'll be able to spy on stupid kids like all the ones out there. I'll be able to find out what they like and don't like. That way, I'll get them all hooked on even more of my super-addictive games!'

'How close are you to controlling WorldEye?' asked Zac.

'One line of computer code away.'

Jimmy Shady consulted his notes. 'We know the second-last line is $H=//t+13$, but we haven't cracked the last line yet. The kids I've recruited today are doing tests right now.'

Zac said nothing.

'Untold riches will be mine! And the funniest part is, I'm using the kids them-selves to get even more kids hooked on my games!' Jimmy Shady laughed an evil laugh.

It was all Zac needed to hear. As casually as he could, Zac stretched his arms up. Just the way he'd planned it, something rolled down his sleeve and into his hand.

A stink bomb.

Zac always kept one up his sleeve, just in case. It wasn't anything clever or high-tech. But as Zac was learning, sometimes the old-fashioned gadgets are the best.

With all his might, Zac chucked the stink bomb at the wall.

It exploded.

Instantly the room filled with gas.

Jimmy Shady coughed and spluttered. So did his goons. The gas smelt worse than 10,000 dog farts!

Zac sprang to his feet. Before anyone knew what was happening, he'd raced out the door.

He'd managed to secretly record Jimmy Shady admitting his evil plan on the mini-video camera in his SpyPad. Zac had all the evidence he needed to arrest Jimmy and stop the hackers cracking the final line of computer code.

But how, in a room crawling with Mind-Lab goons, could one 12-year-old arrest the head of MindLab?

CHAPTER 10

Zac tore through the Games Convention towards the main stage.

With all the monitors and equipment on the stage, the next part of his plan would be easy. As quick as lightning, Zac plugged his SpyPad into the 'Video In' jack on the giant screen.

Zac hit Play. Suddenly, Jimmy Shady's

voice boomed through the Bladesville Town Hall. Everyone stopped what they were doing and looked up. Zac was broadcasting Jimmy Shady's confession for the entire convention to hear.

'Untold riches will be mine! And the funniest part is, I'm using the kids themselves to get even more kids hooked on my games!' Jimmy Shady said.

All across the hall, kids started talking to each other.

'Hear that?'

'The head of MindLab's been messing with gamers!'

'Let's get him! And the hackers!' Zac heard someone yell.

Like a boiling pot about to overflow, the convention erupted. Kids shouted. Game consoles flew through the air.

It was chaos! The gamers stormed Jimmy Shady's glass office. Within moments, he was captured and handcuffed. Soon he was driven away in a police car.

Zac's plan had worked perfectly. His mission was complete – thanks to the kids!

Suddenly, Zac heard his SpyPad bleep.

He'd have to hurry if he was going to make it home in time to put the bins out. But how on earth would he get there? His invisible fighter jet had been stolen by the hackers. There just wasn't time to search for it.

Zac paced up and down outside Jimmy Shady's office. It was empty now, sealed off with black and yellow crime-scene tape. There was something on the floor, though. Something that looked like…yes!

Car keys.

When no-one was looking, Zac grabbed the keys. He wasn't going to *steal* Jimmy Shady's car. More like *borrow* it. Just to drive himself to Bladesville airport so he could get a flight home.

There was always his karaoke hover scooter. But somehow Zac suspected Jimmy Shady would have something much faster, much cooler, he could use.

Zac raced to the car park outside the

Town Hall. There were hundreds of cars parked there!

Which one was Jimmy Shady's?

A remote unlocking device dangled from the key ring. Zac hit the blipper. He heard the sound of a vehicle door unlocking. But Zac couldn't see which car was unlocking its door and flashing its lights.

Zac tried the remote over and over. But not one of the cars seemed to be opening. Zac looked around in frustration.

It was then that he saw it. There was a heli-pad on the roof of the Town Hall. With a brand-new, ultra-light stealth helicopter parked and waiting.

Zac tried the remote once again.

The helicopter's lights came on!

The doors opened!

He'd found his ride home.

As Zac ran towards the heli-pad, a brief doubt flickered through his mind. He'd never actually flown a helicopter before. Then again, in the past 24 hours, he'd piloted a fighter jet, won a gaming comp, hooned around on a hover scooter, sung karaoke and busted Jimmy Shady.

I reckon I can handle a helicopter, thought Zac to himself.

THE END